Troubles with Bubbles

Written by Frank B. Edwards
Illustrated by John Bianchi

sandbox

slide

mud

I am dirty. I want to be clean.

Go to the tub and scrub
with soap and water.

We are dirty.
We want to be clean.

Go to the tub and scrub
with soap and water.

We are dirty.
We want to be clean.

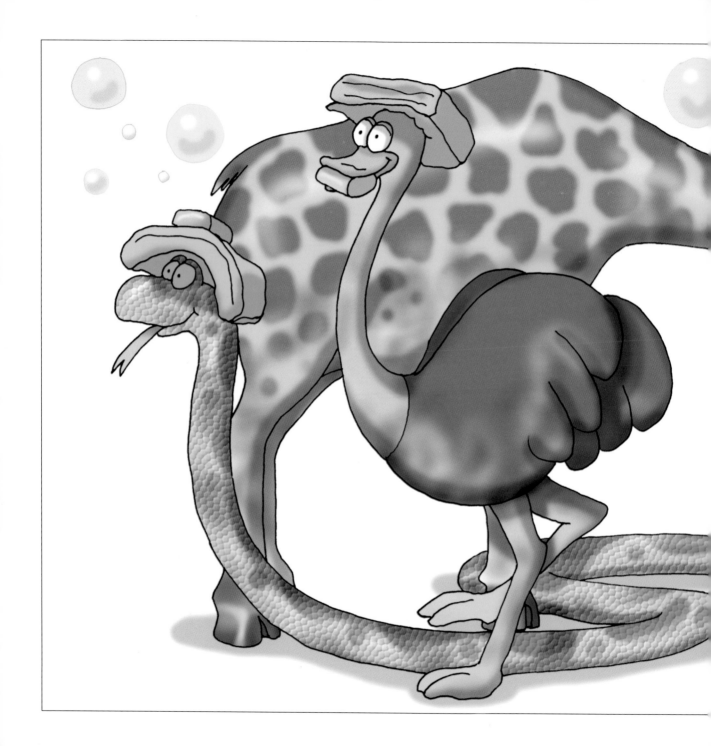

Go to the tub and scrub
with soap and water.

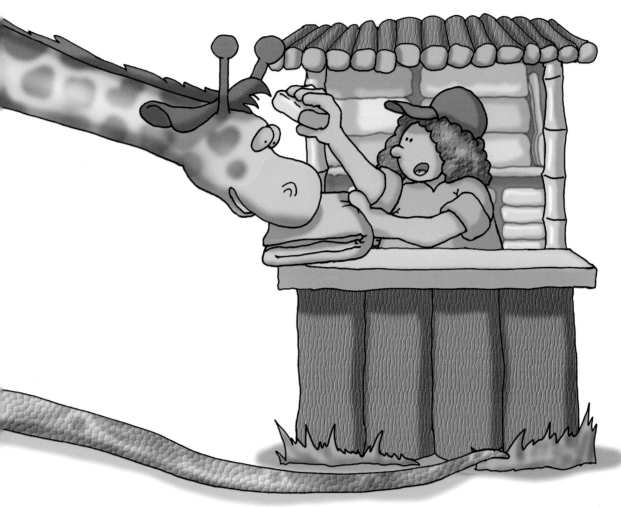

We are dirty.
We want to be clean.

Go to the tub and scrub
with soap and water.

You have used too much soap.

Thank you.
Now we are clean.

The End